I Love My Mummy

igloobooks

Early in the morning, I tiptoe into Mummy's room and wake her with hugs and kisses.

"Good morning, Mummy," I say, as we snuggle up together and watch the sun rise.

Mummy and me make pancakes for breakfast.

I love it when she flips them high in the air.

I help Mummy to stir the mixture.

When it's nearly gone, I get to lick the spoon.

Soon, it's time to get dressed and Mummy helps me find my blue trousers and red top.

Sometimes, I do silly things to make Mummy smile.
"Socks don't go on your ears!" she says, laughing.

I love going to the park with Mummy. I like it best when she pushes me on the swing.

I love to whoosh through the air as high as
I can go and shout, "Again, again!"

Sometimes, Mummy and me have a picnic.

We spread out our rug and eat yummy sandwiches.

As a surprise, I pick Mummy some pretty flowers.

I know she likes the red ones best.

Mummy and me have fun painting pictures.

We splodge the paint onto the paper with our brushes.

When we are finished, Mummy hangs my best paintings on the fridge, so everyone can see them.

When my clothes are mucky, Mummy puts them in the washing machine and I watch them go round and round.

On the washing line, the clothes flip and flap in the wind.
I pretend the sheet is a sail on a pirate ship.

Mummy is really good at cooking. She always makes me tasty things to eat for dinner.

I try to eat all of my vegetables because Mummy says they will help me grow up big and strong.

At bath time, Mummy fills my bath with soapy bubbles.
I love to make the bubbles go POP!

When I'm clean, Mummy scoops me up and rubs
me dry with a soft, fluffy towel.

Mummy helps me to put on my softest, most comfy pyjamas, so I'm all snug and warm.

"Come on," says Mummy, "it's time for a bedtime story.
Which book shall we read tonight?"

We cuddle up in bed and read together. Mummy does
all the funny voices and makes me giggle.

By the last page, I feel very sleepy, so Mummy tucks
me up and turns on my night light.

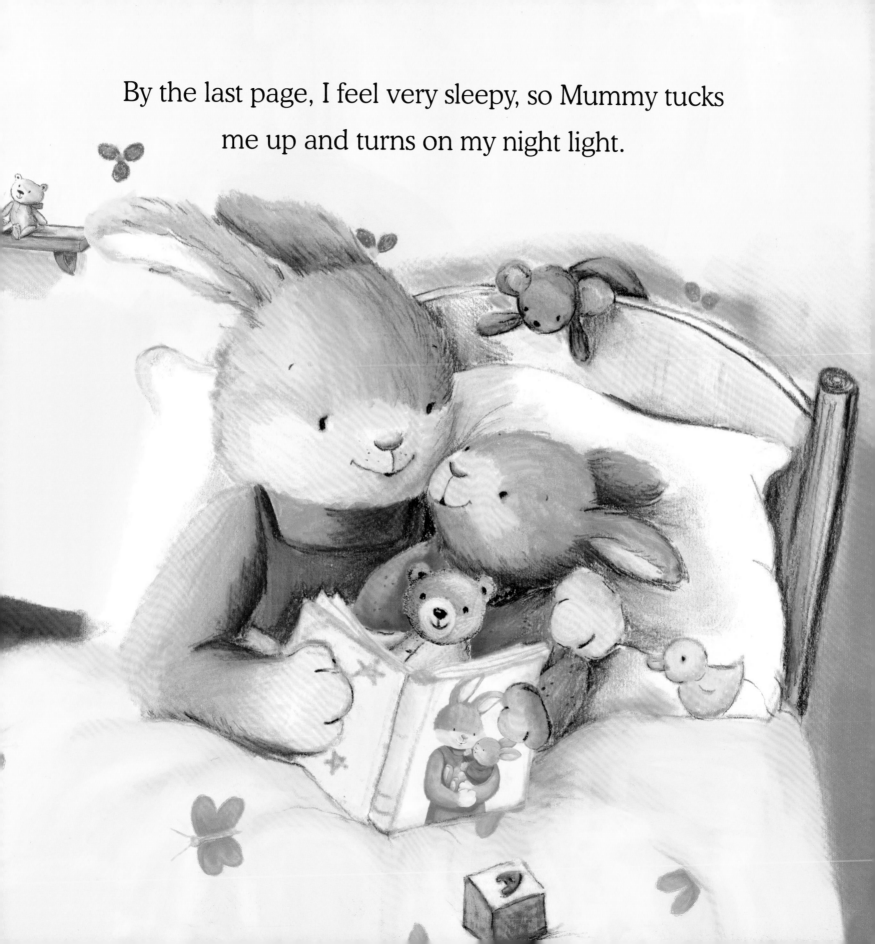

"Goodnight, sleep tight," says Mummy, kissing my head.
I love my mummy. She's the best mummy in the whole world.